All We Know of Heaven

by

Peter Crowther

D0807653

Published in Great Britain by Barrington Stoke Ltd
10 Belford Terrace, Edinburgh EH4 3DQ
Copyright © 2001 Peter Crowther
First published in different form in *The Longest Single Note*
(Cemetary Dance Publications, 1999)

The moral right of the author has been asserted in
accordance with the Copyright, Designs and Patents Act 1988
ISBN 1-84299-032-2
Printed by Polestar AUP Aberdeen Ltd

A Note from the Author

All We Know Of Heaven is, in a way, about King Arthur and his enchanted sword. But it's set in the present, there are no knights in it and no Merlin the wizard. And the only round table is the one in Adam Best's house. So, you may well ask, how does King Arthur come into it?

Well, it's a few days before Christmas – a very unhappy Christmas for Adam and his dad – and Adam's school class are learning about the legend of King Arthur. In that story, Adam sees something ...

But I'm not going to tell you any more or there would be no point in your reading the book! So I'll just say this: what you're about to read is a tale about great strength and great goodness. It's about love and loss, and the sadness that love and loss can bring. It's scary and it's exciting and, in the end, things work out OK ... kind of. In other words, it's about life ... after all, what else matters?

Happy reading!

For Kathleen Crowther

1921-2000

Contents

Chapter 1

A Special Week

The week leading up to Christmas was going to be a turning point in Adam Best's life. But, of course, he didn't know this yet.

In fact, right now, all Adam knew was that the weather was cold and wet. And his father had told him that the chap on the TV had said it was going to be even colder and wetter by the time it got to Christmas Day.

Adam didn't bother to watch the weather on TV or listen to the radio news or read the newspaper like his father did. But there were some programmes he did like to watch and he listened to the radio now and again.

He watched the music channels, MTV and VH1, since his dad had organised Cable to come into the house on South Drive. He listened to Radio One in the morning when he was getting ready for school.

And he read a bit too. He bought *X Men* comics when he could afford them.

But none of that told him what the weather was going to be like in Harrogate during the week leading up to Christmas. So the first he knew about the cold snap was when his father was leaving the house for work.

"Make sure you wrap up warm today, lovey," his father shouted from the car through the open window. "The chap on the TV said it's going to drop below freezing point."

Adam gave his dad the thumbs-up sign to show he'd heard and waved the car off up the street. He watched as he always did until it got to the top, turned onto Leeds Road and vanished. Then he went back inside, put his breakfast things in the dishwasher and brushed his teeth before heading off to school.

Adam's mother, Grace, always used to call him 'lovey' before the accident. And since the accident, Adam's father had taken up the habit. Adam understood that. It was as if she was still at home with them instead of being cooped up in the hospital.

Adam pulled the front door closed and tested it, to make sure it was properly shut, the way his mother had always taught him. Then he pulled up the collar of his coat and stepped out onto the drive into the icy air.

The weather was so cold that it took his breath away. The freezing wind battered his face and neck, and thick drops of rain stung his cheeks and made his lips and nose feel like they were frozen into solid lumps.

Turning out of South Drive onto Park Road, Adam stuck out his tongue to taste the rain. Mr Stevens had told them in geography about rain being water pulled up from far out at sea and carried across to Harrogate by the clouds. But it didn't taste salty. Maybe the clouds absorbed the salt.

He turned onto West Road and came at last to the school crossing.

For once in his life, it was almost a relief to see the school traffic warden, Mr Newman with his giant lollipop. It meant he would soon be out of the rain and into the warmth of the school building.

As he waited for Mr Newman to stop the traffic, Adam screwed up his eyes against the wind. The school gates and fencing loomed at the end of Cherry Avenue. Against their dark shapes Adam could now see that the rain was starting to turn into snow. It swirled and drifted in front of him and piled up against the wall, where nobody's feet could disturb it.

"Hi there!"

Adam looked around and saw the grinning face of Johnny Parks. He nodded and said, "Do you think the snow's going to lie?"

"My mum says it's too wet to lie. But I think she's just hoping it won't." Johnny turned around and waved to his mum as she drove past. She returned his wave without taking her eyes off the road ahead of her.

"Why is she hoping the snow doesn't lie?" Adam asked, as he watched Mrs Parks's car come to a halt behind a lot of other cars at the traffic lights, their exhaust pipes puffing smoke into the cold air.

"Because she's worried she'll have to take me sledging." Johnny leaned forward and looked along the pavement edge to where another boy was ambling along, as though it was a sunny day in July. "You OK, Simon?" he shouted.

Simon Grant waved a gloved hand and started to run towards them. "Worn out," he told them with a loud puff as he reached the crossing. "It's taken me ages to get here this morning."

Old Mr Newman sidled into the centre of the road. He held up his lollipop sign and made frantic signals with his free hand for the boys to hurry. "Come on, come on," he snapped. "Can't keep the traffic held up all day." He mouthed a few curses which were carried away by the wind, but the boys knew what he was saying.

"You shouldn't swear at us," Johnny said as they started across the road.

"I'll do more than swear at you," Mr Newman said, "if you give me any more of your lip." His words were mumbled into the thick scarf around his neck.

Simon bent forward and lifted his coat away from his bottom as they reached the old man, blowing a raspberry with his mouth. Adam and Johnny laughed but started to run as Mr Newman reached out for them. He just failed to grab Johnny's coat collar. A car horn blared from behind them.

"Just you be patient!" Mr Newman shouted. He hadn't forgotten the boys. He made sure they were safe and then moved back to the side of the road. He started to wave the cars on again. Adam watched them gain speed, their engines roaring, only to have to slow down again at the next red light.

When he looked across at Mr Newman, Adam thought he saw the old man smile at him, give him a wink and a little shake of his head. But it must just have been the wind and the snow making Mr Newman twitch.

"Come on," Johnny shouted as he ran into the wind, which blasted down Cherry Avenue. His voice drifted away over his shoulder sounding strange and distant.

"Yeah," Simon said as he hitched the strap of his bag further onto his shoulder, "my brother says when it's really cold it can freeze your nose and make it drop off. And you'd end up spending Christmas in hospital."

"Like my mum," Adam said. He wondered if the nurses in the hospital would have a tree and lights and hand out presents to all the patients.

Simon shouted after Johnny who was rapidly vanishing. "Hey, Parks! Wait for us!" But Johnny didn't seem to have heard him.

"Come on," Simon said to Adam. They both started to run. Their pounding feet splattered muddy slush over each others legs.

Chapter 2
Not Just A Treat

It was almost the end of term. Lessons had already started to wind down. It was still a surprise, however, when Miss Ridge started her Monday morning English lesson by telling them that she was going to read them a book.

Everyone cheered. "It's not just a *treat*," she shouted, over the noise. "It's to do with next term's project."

Everyone groaned. Adam, who was at the front of the class, looked around to see rows of frowning faces topped by thick thatches of hair – golden, brown and black and all as messy as birds' nests. In the desk right behind Adam, Jimmy Bell pulled a thick piece of snot out of his left nostril, rolled it between his fingers and popped the resulting small grey ball into his mouth.

"Save some for lunchtime, James," Miss Ridge said as she lifted out her chair from behind the big desk and plopped it down right in front of Adam.

"That's another piece of brain you'll never use, Jimmy," Christine Reed shouted. Everyone laughed.

"That's enough from you, Christine," Miss Ridge said. Her eyes narrowed as she looked in Christine's direction.

Adam liked Miss Ridge. She seemed different to the other teachers and it wasn't just that she was younger.

The fact was that, in many ways, Miss Ridge reminded Adam of his mum. Her hair was the same lovely dark brown colour as his mum's, catching the light and shining. He would sometimes think about what it would feel like to run his hand through Miss Ridge's hair ... the way he had run his hand through his mum's hair when he used to sit on her knee before bedtime.

One of Miss Ridge's front teeth stuck out a bit, so that sometimes, when her mouth was closed, there would be a faint glint of tooth on her lower lip. Just like there was now. Adam's mum's teeth stuck out slightly too, and she was always saying, before the accident, that she would have to get them fixed sometime. But Adam's dad wouldn't hear of it. He said her teeth were cute. Whenever Dad said that, which was often, Adam's mum would tell him he was daft.

Miss Ridge clapped her hands loudly. "All right class, let's settle down now." She sat down and smoothed out her skirt.

Ben Morris had told a small group of mates that once she'd sat with her legs so far apart that he'd been able to see right up her skirt to her pants. "I tell you," he'd said, glancing around to make sure that they were all listening, "she wears really fancy ones."

Of course, the news spread around the male members of his class like one of those forest wildfires in Australia they had been showing on the TV news. Before long, there was a steady *plip plop* of rubbers and pencils and rulers falling to the floor, quickly followed by a lot of bending down and crawling around to find them, while the boys tried hard to see up Miss Ridge's skirt.

But not Adam. The reason was that she reminded him so much of his mother. And Adam hated to think of anybody trying to get a look at his mum's private parts. It was even worse now that she was in hospital and couldn't do anything for herself.

In fact, the idea made him so angry that he thought he'd just have to smack anybody in the mouth if he ever caught them trying it. This was the way he always felt when he went with his dad to visit her in hospital and some doctor arrived who wanted to check her over.

Check her over! *Yeah*, Adam thought, *doctors can look wherever they like.* Each time Adam and his dad were asked by the doctor to step out of the room, Adam felt angry. The doctor would pull screens around the bed and get to work. And, of course, Adam's mum could never object.

In fact, Adam's mum could never object to anything any more.

****

"Adam? Are you with us?" Miss Ridge said sharply.

Adam's eyes focused on his teacher. She was looking right at him, holding up a book. He sat up straight and nodded, feeling his cheeks go red.

"Daydreaming, Adam?"

He nodded. "Sorry, Miss."

Miss Ridge gave him a little smile, then looked over Adam's head at the rest of the class. "So," she said, waving the book in her hand. I'll read you the title – *The Acts of King Arthur And His Noble Knights: From The Winchester Manuscripts of Thomas Mallory.*"

"That's not a title, it's a whole sentence – a life sentence!" Meesha Shameel muttered loudly. The whole class sniggered. Meesha liked to play the class clown. There was no doubt, at least as far as his classmates were concerned, that he would be following in the footsteps of Eddie Murphy and Jim Carrey. Even Miss Ridge had to laugh at him sometimes, though she tried to do this without anyone noticing. They all did, of course.

But this time, Miss Ridge was not amused.

"You think you're so clever, Meesha," she said.

"Thank you, Miss," Meesha responded without so much as a second's pause.

More sniggers. Still Miss Ridge did not smile.

"She's calling you a smart arse," Christine Reed said loudly. "You idiot!"

The sniggering grew to a roar.

Miss Ridge clapped her hands again and turned to Christine. "Christine, if I have to speak to you again this lesson, I will send *you* out of the room."

"Yes, Miss." Christine looked down at her desk lid, but she was smiling.

"Is that clear, Christine?"

Christine looked up and nodded. "Yes, Miss."

But Adam missed all of this. His mind had stuck on what Meesha had said about the book's title.

Chapter 3
Life Sentence

Life sentence.

Those were the words that the doctor had used to Adam's father last week. They went every weekend to visit his mum in hospital. Adam only went there on a Saturday and Sunday afternoon. His dad insisted that Adam should wear his neatest clothes. They would drive up to the hospital in Wetherby Road and sit beside Adam's mum for an hour or so.

During the whole visit, Adam's father would hold his wife's hand and just stare at her. Or he would stare at the stack of screens and dials on the table by her side. He gazed at the little green lines and displays. Every now and then they would *bleep*.

Adam had not been with his mum and dad when the huge lorry had crossed from the other side of the motorway and hit their car. But there were times that he almost wished he had been. Those were the times when he lay in his bed in the darkness and listened to his dad pacing up and down beneath him in the lounge. And he knew why. He knew that his Dad couldn't face coming upstairs to the empty bed he used to share with Adam's mum.

Every so often, when Adam had been able to stay awake until his dad came to bed, he would hear him sobbing in the next room. The first time he heard this, Adam got out of bed and tip-toed silently to his parents' bedroom. He peered around the door and saw his father sitting on Mum's side of the bed with his back to Adam, whispering to her photograph. It was a strange and lonely sound.

Adam never got out of bed again in the middle of the night. But he still heard his father whispering his mum's name again and again, like it was some kind of spell.

Adam thought about his mum and dad a lot. He thought about them when he was meant to be listening to Miss Ridge. His mind would drift away from the lesson and then come back with a jolt.

Today was no different. He had lost track of what Miss Ridge was saying.

"John Steinbeck wrote this book. He was born in California in the United States of America, in 1902," Miss Ridge said. Adam wondered what on earth she was talking about. "And he was awarded the Nobel Prize for Literature in 1962." She rested the book on her knees, its cover still facing the class.

Adam stared at the book's cover. It showed a knight in armour, sitting on a horse and waving his sword. The horse wore what looked like a green and brown patchwork bedcover, all the way from the tip of its tail to the point of its nose. The knight's helmet made him look brave. Even the horse looked brave. Adam wondered what it must have been like to be a knight in the days of King Arthur.

He glanced around at the other children and saw that they were settling down to listen. When he turned back, Adam saw that Miss Ridge had opened the book and was reading from it.

"... a great block of marble. And in the marble was set a steel anvil in which a sword was driven. In letters of gold was written:

*WHOEVER PULLS THIS SWORD FROM THIS
STONE AND ANVIL IS KING OF ALL ENGLAND."*

Her voice boomed as she read out what
was written on the block of marble. She
lowered the book again and looked at the
children.

"*The people were amazed,*" Miss Ridge
went on, "*and they carried the news of the
miracle to the Archbishop, who said, 'Go back
into the church and pray to God. And let no
man touch the sword until High Mass is sung'.
And this they did, but when the service was
over, all the lords went to look at the stone
and the sword. And some tried to draw out
the blade. But no-one could move it.*"

Some of the class were looking puzzled
and Miss Ridge stopped to explain. "Everyone
thought it was hopeless trying to pull out the
sword. But the Archbishop knew that the
right person at the right time would have the
strength. '*The man is not here who will draw*

21

this sword, said the Archbishop, *but do not doubt that God will make him known.'"*

Miss Ridge lifted back a piece of her hair that had fallen over her eyes. Adam watched her with his mouth open. *No-one could move it.* The words reminded him of something someone had said. But who and where?

When Miss Ridge started to read again about King Arthur and the sword, Adam was no longer listening. Instead, he was thinking back to the first time he and his dad had visited the hospital.

Chapter 4

Intensive Care

Adam had relived the first visit to the hospital many times over the months that he and his father had been living alone. It was a whole month after the accident, but his father was still limping badly.

He wore a bandage and a large pad over his right eye, where his face had hit the back of Adam's mum's head.

When the lorry crashed into them, Adam's mum was thrown into the driver's side of the car – which was when her head hit Dad's face. Then she bounced back onto her own side. Their car had skidded crazily across into the fast lane where it had been hit by a speeding sports car. The passenger side of their car had been crushed like a paper cup.

Their car had then been pushed even further out across the motorway where it had crashed with the metal barrier. The car's wheel arch had pushed through the engine block, thrusting the brake up off the floor. At the time, Adam's dad's foot had been pressing on that brake in a desperate attempt to control the car.

Adam's dad was very badly hurt, but he got off lightly compared with his wife.

Adam's dad hadn't allowed Adam to visit the hospital at first because Grace Best's face had been so badly hurt. But finally the day came and Adam made himself look really smart for the occasion. He even bought a small bunch of red roses with his own pocket money from the market stall in town. The man on the stall knew all about the accident and he didn't want to take Adam's money. But Adam insisted.

Later that same afternoon, Adam walked into Harrogate District Hospital with his silent father, listening to the sound of their shoes clacking on the polished floor.

They walked through the large glass doors, past a round reception desk and along a long corridor to the lifts. Adam's dad crushed out his cigarette in a sand tray. He was smoking a lot these days. He pressed the lift button and waited, his hands in his pockets.

The lift arrived with a *ting!* and they got in.

Adam's dad pressed the button for the fourth floor and leaned against the back wall of the lift. The doors closed with a *shhh!* and Adam felt a jerking movement as the lift started up.

The *ting!* of the lift arriving on the fourth floor seemed much quieter than when they had been waiting on the ground floor for it to arrive. The doors slid open to reveal a metal sign on the wall. The sign read:

INTENSIVE CARE

Adam's father put an arm around his shoulder. He hardly ever did that nowadays. He guided Adam out of the lift and they went along to a reception desk which was cluttered with papers and clipboards. A girl who didn't seem much older than some of the girls in their last year at Adam's school smiled warmly and made a big thing out of Adam's roses. Adam kept silent, longing for all this to be over. He wanted to see his mum.

He watched his dad sign in the book on the counter and then followed him through two swing doors into a short corridor. Halfway along, Adam's dad stopped. They were outside a room. Adam looked at the door and saw that it had the name 'Best' written on a piece of card that had been slipped into a metal holder.

"Come on, son," Adam's dad said. He stood up very straight and drew in a deep breath. "Let's see how your mum's doing today." And they walked into the room.

Although Adam had been told what he might find there, it was not at all as he expected.

For many lonely nights that followed this first visit, Adam tried to picture what he had been expecting or even hoping to find. Whatever it was, it wasn't what he discovered when he walked into his mum's hospital room that Sunday afternoon in October, when the first leaves of autumn were already beginning to fall.

It was not his mum at all.

Stretched out on a metal bed, thin arms attached by wires and tubes to a host of blinking and dripping machines. It looked hardly human. Adam blinked to himself, first because it was so absurd that anyone could try to make him believe that this was his mum … then, he blinked again, this time with tears in his eyes, as he saw that it *was* her.

Her mouth was slightly open, her cheeks were sunken and bony. Her eyes were tightly closed. Neither her face nor her body moved. Maybe she was sleeping. What could she be dreaming of now, if she dreamed at all? Lonely memories might drift through her mind, lost hopes and failed intentions. Adam wondered if she remembered him at all.

On her head, where her hair had been shaved, was a taped wire which led into a stack of display panels which looked like his dad's stereo set-up. Green blip lines flashed across the displays. A second wire was attached to Mum's left arm. It also ran into the equipment.

Adam watched the blips on the screens. And he listened.

Bleep ... bleep ... bleep ...

There was a constant noise from the recording machines – he wondered if his mother were trying to send him messages through the machinery.

Adam looked away from the displays and, for the first time, saw something attached to his mum's neck. It was the biggest, meanest looking tube of all ... a large one which came out of a machine standing away from the others beside the bed. It seemed to plunge into his mum's throat.

Adam reached toward it without thinking.

"No!" A voice behind him said firmly.

Adam turned around and came face to face with a nurse in a blue uniform. She was older than the one they had seen on the way in, and she looked at him with a finger raised in warning. She had been sitting behind the door all the time but Adam hadn't seen her. He had been too intent on looking at his mum.

The woman's face slipped into a gentle smile and she reached out a hand and ruffled Adam's hair.

"No-one can move that, young man," she said.

Adam looked around and saw his dad's glazed eyes watching him. Then he dropped the neat bunch of red roses onto his mother's unmoving feet and ran to his father. They hugged each other and cried together.

But all that was weeks ago.

Chapter 5
The Strength To Prevail

Adam stared across at the classroom window and watched the snow falling outside. Miss Ridge's voice went on.

"*And King Arthur took hold of the sword by its handle*," Miss Ridge said, looking up from the book, "*and easily pulled it out of the stone.*" She closed the book and looked at the class. "Has anyone got anything they want to say?"

She tapped on the desk to attract Adam's attention. "Are you with us, Adam?" she said. He blinked and looked around. The other kids in his class were watching him. He cleared his throat and tried to smile. "Yes, Miss," he said, trying to keep calm.

"Don't tell me you're thinking about lunch already," she teased.

Some of the boys sniggered at the back of the room and Adam thought he heard someone fart. The sound made him want to laugh out loud, but he tried hard to keep his mouth straight.

"Do you think it's funny if I have to remind you where you are every five minutes?" Miss Ridge asked.

Adam shook his head. "No, Miss."

"Then try to pay attention please."

At that moment, when the rest of the class were turning their faces away from him, Miss Ridge gave Adam a gentle smile. *It's OK*, the smile seemed to say to him, *I know what you're going through*. And then she spoke to the whole class. "So, what's the message we get from the story of King Arthur and the sword in the stone?"

Adam saw a hand shoot up a couple of desks away.

"Yes, Sally," Miss Ridge said.

"Does it mean that it's good to be strong?"

Miss Ridge smiled and nodded, though Adam saw that she was frowning a little. "Well, yes it does, Sally. But it doesn't just mean that your body is strong – like Tarzan's." She held up her right arm and flexed the muscle ... and then beat her chest. Everyone laughed as she returned her arm to her lap.

33

"It means strength of mind, too," Miss Ridge said. "It means …" She searched for the right words. "It means that if you're in the right, you will prevail."

"Prevail?" little Peter Bateman asked.

Miss Ridge glanced across at him. "I'm sorry, Peter. 'Prevail' means to overcome your difficulties, to get there in the end. It means to be –"

Out in the corridor, the bell for lunch rang loudly. Papers were shuffled together and desk lids were lifted and slammed shut again, as books were slipped away out of sight.

"We'll continue with the story after break," Miss Ridge told them, raising her voice over the growing noise and chatter.

Within a few seconds, the classroom had cleared as the children rushed to be the first at the school shop. Only Adam and a smiling Miss Ridge remained.

Adam got up from his desk and walked over to Miss Ridge.

"How are things at home, Adam?"

"OK," Adam said. "Things are fine." He picked up Miss Ridge's book and looked at the front cover more closely.

"You like that story, Adam?"

Adam nodded.

"Yes, it's one of *my* favourites." She ran a hand through her hair, just the way Adam's mum used to do, and got up from her chair.

Adam could feel her watching him but he didn't say anything.

"Was there something you wanted to ask me, Adam?"

Adam shifted his weight from foot to foot. "What were you going to say?"

Miss Ridge frowned though her smile remained. "What was I going to say *when?*"

"When the bell went. You were telling Peter what 'prevail' meant. You said that it meant to overcome your difficulties ... and then you added 'it means to be ...' but you never finished."

"Ah," she said. "I think I was going to say 'to be a winner even if the odds are against you'. Is that what you wanted to know?"

"I think so," he said. "It's to win your own battles, isn't it." Adam held out the book and Miss Ridge took it from him. He walked quickly out of the classroom leaving Miss Ridge with a sad and puzzled expression on her face.

Chapter 6
A Night Out

Just after lunch on Wednesday, school finished for the Christmas break. It was the 22nd of December.

On the 23rd, it started to snow again.

Adam spent the day playing round at Johnny Parks's house.

In the morning they played games on the computer. For lunch they had chicken sandwiches, crisps and Coca Cola, and spent the afternoon in Johnny's room looking through his piles of comics. Johnny had a lot of comics that Adam hadn't even seen. Before they knew it – with Johnny telling Adam all about the different storylines in great detail – it was time for tea.

Mrs Parks came in and said that, if Adam's father didn't mind, maybe Adam would like to have tea with them and then sleep over.

"And maybe we'll get out a video to watch later," she added. "Would you like that, Adam?"

Adam couldn't help himself. "Oh wow!"

"Johnny?" she said. "I just realised I hadn't checked with you. Are you OK with Adam staying over?"

"Oh *double* wow!" Johnny shouted and both he and Adam fell back onto the bed and started to laugh.

"OK," Mrs Parks said with a chuckle, "I'll take it that means yes. But phone and let your father know, Adam," she added as she was leaving Johnny's bedroom. "If it's OK, tell him I'll take you home around 11 o'clock tomorrow morning."

"What video are we watching?" Johnny called after her.

"I'll call Daddy and ask him to pick one up on his way home," Johnny's mum shouted from the stairs.

Adam phoned home from the telephone in the Parks's hall.

It was the answering machine. *Hello*, his father's voice said. *Grace, James and Adam Best can't take your call right now. But leave a message and we'll call you back.* The phone bleeped and Adam recorded his message.

"Dad, it's me," Adam said. "Mrs Parks says I can stay over at Johnny's – I'm having tea here and we're going to watch a video and stuff. I'll be home in the morning around 11 o'clock." He looked around to see if anyone was listening and then added, in a whisper, "Love you."

He placed the phone down and stared at it.

From the kitchen he heard the radio with a posh voice reading the news and the sounds of Johnny's mum moving around, banging pots and turning on the water in the sink.

Adam glanced up at the window by the front door and saw the snow falling. He walked across and looked out. It was dark and the cars were driving slowly down Ripon Road. The snow lay thick on the pavements.

He turned and stared again at the phone. The words ran through Adam's head.

Grace, James and Adam Best can't take your call right now.

The kitchen door opened and Mrs Parks looked out into the hall. "Have you called your father, Adam?"

He nodded. "He's not in," he said. "He goes to see Mum after work. He'll be at the hospital."

Mrs Parks smiled. It was a strangely sad little smile. "I'm sure it'll be OK," she said, though Adam wasn't sure what she was talking about – his staying over for the night or his mum in hospital – but he nodded.

"Anyway," she said, clapping her hands, "how do you feel about mushrooms? We're going to have a big fry – bacon, sausages, tomatoes ..."

"Can we have baked beans too?"

Mrs Parks threw back her arms. "Of course – baked beans coming right up. Are you happy with the mushrooms?"

"Great!" Adam said trying to sound as keen as he could. In fact Adam didn't like mushrooms at all, but his mum always told him to take what he was given when he was at a friend's house.

"OK," she said, "you go play with Johnny and I'll give you both a shout when it's ready."

Adam ran up the stairs and Mrs Parks went back into the kitchen.

At the top of the first long flight of stairs, Adam stopped. With his hand holding onto the banister, he looked back at the phone.

Adam and James Best can't take your call right now, a voice said in his head. But this time it wasn't his father speaking. "What about Mum?" whispered Adam. *Your Mum's very poorly, Adam*, the voice said. It sounded as though the voice wanted to add something but it didn't. The silence it left behind had a sound all of its own.

Chapter 7
Christmas Eve

Adam didn't go home the next morning.

It had snowed very hard in the night and Mrs Parks said that if Adam wanted to stay until late afternoon she'd take him and Johnny sledging down in the Valley Gardens. Johnny's dad had bought him a new sledge and so Adam could use the old one. Adam called home and spoke to his dad and his dad said that was fine. He'd look forward to seeing him around tea-time.

The day was a wonderful day.

Even Johnny's mum had a go sledging. She had Johnny's new sledge and Adam led the way on the old one. She wasn't very good at it though and, without even getting half way down the full run on the long slope, she gave up and handed the sledge back to Johnny. She clapped and yelled as the two of them tore down the slope, time after time, until it was time to go home.

They dropped Adam off at the end of his street. He said his goodbyes and Mrs Parks gave him a big kiss on the side of his face.

"Have a great Christmas," she said to him, and she put her arms round him and hugged him close. Her eyes looked a little watery – Adam thought she might have caught a bit of a chill from falling into the snow so many times. Or was she trying not to cry?

"I will," he promised her. At the gate he turned to wave.

Thank them for having you, lovey, a soft voice whispered in Adam's head. It was his mother's voice.

"Thanks for having me," he shouted.

Mrs Parks gave a wave as she wound up the window of the car and drove off. It was almost dark.

Adam walked up the path to his front door.

He lifted the mat on the bottom step and felt for the key. As he let himself into the house, he could hear voices coming from the kitchen.

"What can I tell you, Jim?" someone was saying.

"Don't speak too loud," Adam's dad said. "Adam'll be home soon."

Adam slipped his shoes off and stood against the living room door.

He could hear the sound of food being prepared in the kitchen. It was a sound that was so much a part of his home and so much a part of his mother's place in the home, that, just for a few seconds, he thought that maybe the accident had never happened. It was a dream or something. Maybe he would walk into the kitchen right now and there would be his mum, cooking supper.

She'd see him and she'd run right over and lift him up, spin him around. *Here's my big boy home from his adventures*, she would say. And she'd kiss him, kiss and hug him the way that Mrs Parks had tried to kiss and hug him – the way all mothers kiss and hug their children – and all around them would be the sounds and the sights and the smells of their everyday happiness together.

But Adam knew that this wasn't to be. He stood and listened.

"Just tell me the truth, Phil," Adam's dad said.

"I'm telling you the truth."

It was Phil Garnett, Adam's dad's oldest and closest friend. Phil was also their doctor.

"Grace isn't coming home for Christmas," Phil said. "She isn't coming home for New Year. She isn't coming home for Easter or the summer holidays or ..."

"OK, OK, OK," Adam's dad said, raising his voice. "Are you telling me there's no chance at all? I don't think I could take that, I really don't."

Phil said nothing.

"I mean," Adam's dad said, his voice lower now, "she's still breathing. And they told me ..."

"Well, OK, yes. There's a chance. One chance in a million – maybe a billion – that Grace will get better. But I'm telling you that it's one chance. And even then ..." His voice trailed off.

"Even then what?"

"Well, even then she may not ... she may not be the way she was before."

"But she's breathing!"

"It's the machine that breathes for her ... through the tube that they inserted. It's not Grace breathing, it's the machine. The tube goes all the way down her throat and into her lung. It inflates and deflates her lung – which is what you and I do by ourselves, without any help at all. It's clever but it's only a machine. It's not Grace."

Adam heard glasses clink and a muffled, "No thanks, Jim. I'm on duty tonight."

Another clink sounded and Phil said, "And that's not all. She has drugs to relax her muscles and stop her fighting the machine; she has more drugs to keep her from pain and still more to help her sleep."

"Oh no more, Phil, no ..."

"No, hear me out, Jim. She has ..."

Adam listened but he didn't understand a lot of the words that Phil was using. But he could understand the basic message. He had known his mum was poorly but this sounded much worse than poorly.

Adam pressed closer to the door to hear Phil's now lowered voice.

"Let her go, Jim. Let her rest."

Adam heard a sob.

"I ... I can't. God help me, I can't," Adam's dad sobbed. "That's like ... that's like you asking me to bury her while she's still alive."

"I know," Phil said and was silent.

Adam put his shoes back on and slipped out of the house. He locked the door and placed the key carefully under the mat again. Then he rang the bell.

"Hi, lovey," Adam's dad said as he opened the door. His eyes looked red. "Have you had a good time at Johnny's?"

"Yeah. Great," he said.

Phil appeared at the living room door. "Hi, Adam."

"Hi, Phil," Adam said.

"Well, got to be going," Phil told them. "Will Jane and I see you tomorrow for Christmas drinks?"

"Indeed you will."

"About 5.30 pm?"

"Fine." Adam's dad ruffled Adam's hair and pulled him close. "I think we'll have opened most of our presents by then, what say you, Adam?"

Adam nodded and stepped back to allow Phil out of the house.

"OK, well ... see you soon, Jim."

"See you soon, Phil. And ... thank you."

They shook hands almost like strangers although they knew each other so well, and then Phil stepped out into the cold.

It seemed to Adam as if their conversation had never happened. Had he imagined it?

He saw that it had started to snow again.

Chapter 8
Visiting Time

Much later, Adam lay safe in bed, alone in his room. He clasped his hands behind his head and stared into the night sky beyond his window. His heart was beating fast. It was now or never.

He slipped from the bed and pulled on his clothes.

Minutes later, he was pulling open the front door.

Outside, the night was cold but at least it had stopped snowing.

As the church clock struck midnight, Adam was running through the darkened streets feeling like a knight of old riding to rescue a maiden fair. He hoped that as there seemed to be so many patron saints for things, there might be one for ten-year-old boys with a mission. And, sure enough, things seemed to be going his way.

At the hospital there was just one man sitting at the reception desk. Adam waited outside, watching him through the full-length windows. The man stood up and went through the door behind him. A couple of minutes later, the man came back with a bunch of files which he set on the desk. The man sat down again and started leafing through papers.

Adam blew into his hands and looked around.

The hospital car park was deserted. There were only a few cars still there and they were covered in snow.

He blew into his hands again and hunched his body against the wall.

"Come on," he whispered to the window pane in front of him. "Come on."

After a few minutes, and just as Adam thought he was going to freeze into a statue, the man stood up again.

Adam moved along to the main door.

As soon as the man went into the back room, Adam pulled open the door and stepped inside.

The warmth was wonderful.

Adam pulled the door closed and tip-toed as quickly as he could past the reception desk and across to the corridor that led to the lifts.

All around him everything looked big. Gigantic. Corridors seemed to stretch on forever and the usually bright lights had been dimmed for the night. Now that he was out of sight from the main desk, he slowed down and moved closer to the wall so that he could slip into a doorway if he saw anyone up ahead. But there wasn't anyone around.

When he turned the corner to the lifts he saw that they were both standing with their doors open ... as if they were waiting for him.

Hello, Adam Best, the one on the left seemed to be saying, *take me.*

No, Adam, the other one whispered, *take me!*

He stepped inside the one on the right and pressed the button for the fourth floor. The lift doors closed with a hiss.

When the doors opened again with a *ting!*, Adam half expected to see a doctor standing waiting for him ... or maybe his father, standing there with his pyjamas on underneath his overcoat. But that was silly, his father couldn't have got down here in front of him. Adam shook his head to chase away such thoughts and peered around the lift door. There was nobody there. The corridor on the fourth floor was silent.

He crept out of the lift and walked along the corridor.

Adam could hear conversation up ahead, where the nurses' little desk area was, and he slowed down. Somebody was talking very softly but he couldn't make out how many there were of them.

He looked around for places to hide. Across the corridor was a dark room with its door half open. Adam could see a Hoover standing just inside the door and, behind the Hoover, piles of what looked like boxes of some kind. He glanced back towards the nurses' desk and then trotted across to the room and stepped inside.

From the safety of the darkness he peered around the door. A nurse came along, walking backwards slowly, nodding and still talking. Her voice sounded urgent but she kept it almost to a whisper. Then the nurse turned around and started walking along the corridor towards Adam.

Adam pulled back and tried to close the door but the Hoover was in the way and he didn't have time to move it. So he pushed it as far as he could to one side and tried to step around it and over the boxes.

His foot clipped one of the boxes but he caught it before it could make any sound.

He held the box close to his chest and hugged the door.

The nurse passed by carrying a metal dish of some kind and never even glanced inside the dark room.

A few seconds later, Adam heard the *sshhh!* of the lift doors.

He waited for a minute or two and then, placing the box carefully back onto the pile, he stepped out into the corridor again.

Staying close to the right-hand wall, Adam carefully moved along until he could see his mum's room across from him, the same piece of card with her name on it stuffed into the metal holder.

Adam closed his eyes and willed himself to listen ... to try to hear if anyone was moving around in there. What if the woman in the blue uniform was still there? Well, if she was, there was nothing he could do about it. And there was no point standing out here in the corridor all night. That way he was sure to get caught. No, he had to move ... and he had to move now.

Adam glanced up the corridor. There was no sign of any movement and no sound of anyone talking. He took a deep breath and stepped out into the middle of the corridor.

Just as he had reached the halfway mark, someone coughed loudly.

Adam froze like a rabbit caught in a car's headlights.

The coughing continued and Adam saw a nurse appear from her desk, but her back was turned towards him. She walked briskly forward and into the room straight ahead. If she had turned then and looked back along the main corridor, the nurse would have seen him. There was nowhere for him to go. But she stepped into the room, leaving the door open.

Adam watched the nurse lean over a bed in the room.

He heard her whispering something in a soothing voice. Then she tucked the sheets around the figure in the bed the way his mum used to tuck the sheets around *him*. But that was way back when he was just a little boy and not a knight in shining armour.

This was it.

When the nurse turned around to come back out of the room at the end of the corridor, she couldn't help but see him.

Adam moved forward, still watching the nurse, and placed a hand on the doorknob of his mum's room.

The nurse whispered something more to the figure in the bed and Adam heard a sleepy, contented groan.

He turned the doorknob, slowly.

Down the corridor, the nurse lifted a clipboard from the bed-head and glanced at it. She returned the clipboard to the bed-head.

The knob had turned as far as it would go. Adam pushed at the door but it seemed to be stuck.

The nurse was starting to turn around.

Adam pushed again.

The door still refused to open.

A soft *beep* sounded.

Somewhere out of sight, where the nurses' desk was, someone said something. Adam couldn't hear exactly what it was but it sounded urgent.

Beep!

He looked down at the door handle, turning it side to side, trying to ignore the *bump! bump!* sound of his heart ... hoping that nobody else could hear it.

Beep!

Just as he heard feet start running, Adam looked up to where the *beep* noise came from and saw a small keypad on the wall just above his head. The keypad was flashing red. It was a word. The word was:

CODE

Code? What did *that* mean?

The running feet were getting louder.

Beep!

The door opened and a nurse stood looking down at him, frowning.

At the same time, a hand rested on his shoulder.

"Hello," a woman's voice said behind him.

Beep!

Another voice, again from behind him, said, "This is a little late for you to be visiting, isn't it?"

Adam turned around. Two more nurses were standing right behind him. One of them was wearing a different uniform. It was purple. The nurse wearing the purple uniform reached across and pressed four of the numbered keys. There was a long *beeeeep!* and then the keypad flashed the word:

ACCEPTED

in red and went blank.

He opened his mouth to say something but only air came out. It was as though he had been struck dumb.

The nurse in his mum's room said, "Do you want to come in?"

He turned to her, gulping air, trying to make sound come out of his mouth, feeling panic rush up his chest ... and then the nurse's smile washed over him. In that instant, Adam knew that this woman had children herself. It was a mother's smile, gentle and understanding.

"Do you want to come and see your mum?" she asked. "Is that it?"

Adam nodded. "Yes," he said. And then he added, "please," the way he knew his mum would want him to do.

Chapter 9

Mum

The light was on in his mum's room but it was dim and somehow a little scary as well.

The light came from two wall lights, one on the wall facing the bed and the other above the chair to the right of where he stood. There was a clipboard lying on the chair and a pen on the floor beside it. Adam thought it was strange that he should see those things before he saw his mum. It was almost as though he didn't want to look.

"Well, there she is," the nurse said, taking hold of Adam's hand and holding it tightly. Her grasp felt comforting somehow. "Did you think we'd hidden her?"

As she led Adam across to the bed, he heard a soft voice in the corridor say that she had rung his father. "He's on his way," the voice said.

The figure on the bed looked the same as it had always looked and Adam felt a pang of guilt that he could ever have thought that it was not his mother.

Her face was the same, although it was a little thinner. And her hair was just as lovely. Adam wanted to speak to her but he knew she wouldn't be able to answer him.

With all the daytime hospital noises silent, Adam could hear his mother breathing. But, although Grace Best's frail chest moved gently up and down, up and down, the sound was not coming from the bed. It was coming from the stack of hi-fi equipment at its side. Something in one of the boxes creaked and sighed ...

Creak

Sigh

"Were you worried about her?" the nurse said.

Adam looked up at the nurse and held his lips tight together. He pulled his hand free and went across to the bed.

Looking down at his mother, Adam watched the movements of her chest beneath the bedclothes. They matched the sounds,

Creak

Sigh

from the machine beside her, slow and tired ... hardly movements at all.

He sat on the bed, next to his mum. This time, he took her hand from where it lay on her chest and held it in his own hand. It felt warm. He bent over and sniffed. It smelled of hospital ... of pills and antiseptic creams and medicines, and of machines and wiring. It smelled of all these and many other things.

But it did not smell of his mother.

The nurse walked over and stood beside him. "Does your dad know you're here?" she asked.

Adam saw from the nurse's face that she knew his father had no idea. And he also knew that the other nurse had rung him.

Creak

Sigh

"What were you going to do?" the nurse asked him.

Adam looked down at his feet. He felt his cheeks and ears go hot, as if they were glowing red in the dim light of his mum's room.

It was a good question. What *had* he been going to do?

Adam looked around at his mum, so still and so silent.

He turned and glanced at the nurse, biting his lip, and then he looked back at his mum's face. It was just the same face as it had always been and yet ... and yet it was different. She was there but not there. It was the face of the woman who had looked after him all of his life ... and it was the face of a woman he had never seen before.

Let her go, Jim. Let her rest.

Phil's words echoed in Adam's head. He saw them like words on a computer screen, shimmering and fading. And then Miss Ridge's face appeared.

It means strength of mind too.

He leaned close to his mother's face and whispered to her.

"Mum? Mummy? It's me."

The nurse moved over next to him and placed a hand on Adam's shoulder. Adam took no notice.

He stared at his mum's eyelids, hoping for the slightest flicker. Did she know who he was? But there was nothing ... nothing except,

Creak

Sigh

The sounds from the machine.

"Mum ... are you there? Can you hear me?" What could he ask her to do as a sign that she knew he was there? "If you can hear me, flick one of your fingers. I'll be able to feel it."

Adam reached over and took hold of her other hand.

Someone behind him whispered something, but the nurse next to him waved a hand. He sat like that for what seemed to be a long time, listening to the machine and holding his mother's hands. There was no flick from any of her fingers. Then he laid her hands down again and looked at his own hands. They were shaking.

In Adam's head, Miss Ridge's voice whispered to him, *it means that if you're in the right you will prevail.*

He picked up his mother's hand in his left hand and held it tight. Then he reached out with his right hand to her throat. His hand was no longer shaking. He took hold of the

73

thick tube, staring wide-eyed at his fingers as they folded around the wide cuff just above the thick patch on his mother's neck.

"Sue!" someone said behind him, and Adam heard steps coming up behind him. The nurse beside him turned sharply and said, "It's OK ... he's OK." Then she leaned over him so that he could see her face without turning his head from his mum. "You're OK, aren't you, Adam?"

Adam said nothing. He was hearing another voice, deep inside his head, saying, *and King Arthur took hold of the sword by its handle, and easily pulled it out of the stone.*

He looked at the hi-fi equipment and all the wires and tubes and blinking lights. But most of all he looked at the single thick tube that went from the lone machine against the wall, the tube that went all the way down Adam's mum's throat. The tube that he now held in his hand.

Creak

Sigh

And in that instant, almost with shock, he knew what he had been going to do.

He had been going to pull out that horrible tube, tear it out of his mum's throat and let her drift with the night and the still silence of the hospital ... let her drift to wherever it was that people went when they were not able to breathe by themselves any more. And he had been going to watch the tube then, watch it, as it twisted around on the floor, pushing and pulling air in and out of nothing instead of in and out of his mum.

He had been going to be a knight, whose cause was true and whose heart was strong. He had been going to do the right thing.

He had been going to set her *free*.

Set

Free

Even the machine seemed to think it was a good idea. But even more than that, he had been going to set *himself and his dad* free.

Adam felt the tears come to his eyes, felt his chin start to wobble and his lips begin to quiver. He put his hands up to his face and started to cry.

"There now," the nurse said. She put her arms around him. "There," she said again.

The hi-fi equipment continued to drone on.

Creak

Sigh

it said, though now it sounded as though it was saying something else, something soothing. What it seemed to say was,

There,

There

in a voice that was so much more familiar than the metallic hiss.

Adam relaxed his body and put his face in the nurse's uniform, felt the tears brimming out of his eyes, making her dress wet. He felt all the tension fall away from his body. And as the tears came and the sound of his crying seemed to fill not only his mum's room but also Adam's whole world, the machine behind him said,

There,

There

But Adam knew that it wasn't the machine at all. Not really.

Chapter 10
Dad

When Adam's dad arrived at the hospital, Adam was drinking a cup of tea and eating ginger biscuits, sitting in a huge, comfy chair at the foot of his mum's bed. The chair was so big that his feet didn't even reach the floor.

Dad's

Here

sighed the machine.

Across the room, the nice nurse – who Adam knew was a mum herself – sat in her own chair, writing on clipboards and in books and looking up every couple of minutes at the equipment. She got out of her chair now and again and walked over to the side of his mum's bed. She didn't seem to do anything much. She just felt Mum's wrist and looked at a little watch.

Adam's father looked into the room and frowned at Adam. Then a nurse came up behind him and asked him if she could have a few words with him. When he came back, he didn't look so angry.

"Let's go home," he said, and he held out his hand to Adam.

When Adam looked across at the nurse, she was smiling at him. But it was such a sad smile that Adam wanted to tell *her* that everything was OK. Wanted to tell her, *There, there.*

On the way out of the hospital, Adam's dad said something strange to the nurse wearing purple. He said, "Do you really think they'll come out? After all, it is Christmas."

The purple nurse didn't look quite as friendly as the nurse in Adam's mum's room, but when his dad said that to her, she looked down at Adam and smiled. *She's a mum, too!* Adam thought. *There were a lot of them around.*

"I can't promise," the nurse said, turning back to face Adam's dad. "But, after all this ..." And she didn't say anything else.

Adam's dad nodded and thanked her and then, taking hold of Adam's hand again, they went out of the hospital. As they went through the reception area, the man behind the desk shook his head at Adam – as though Adam had done something wrong – but Adam couldn't think why.

In the car, Adam said, "Sorry, Dad."

His dad patted his knee. "Nothing to say sorry for, lovey," he said. Then he said, "You just needed to see her, eh?"

Adam wondered how to answer that as he watched the road through the windscreen. It was dark and silent and very lonely. There were no other cars anywhere. "I just wanted ..." he began.

I just wanted to pull that flipping pipe out of Mum's throat ... I just wanted her back home with us ... I just wanted us to be a family again ... and if I couldn't have Mum back, then ...

"I just wanted to see her," he said at last.

"I know," Adam's dad said. "I know."

****

It was almost two o'clock when they got home and, in spite of all the excitement, Adam gave a great yawn.

The night seemed so big and so silent. He stood for a few seconds when they had got out of the car and looked up, feeling himself drawn to the endless blackness and the tiny dots of light scattered across the sky.

"What is it?" Adam's dad said. "What do you see?"

Adam shrugged. "Nothing." He looked across at his dad and shrugged again, kicking at a piece of stone in the driveway. "I was just thinking about Father Christmas and about how he only brings stuff to kids who're good." He looked up again. "He's out there somewhere."

When Adam's dad spoke, his voice sounded croaky. "Yes, and we'd better get you off to bed or he won't bring you anything."

"Dad," Adam said. "I didn't just go to *see* Mum. At the hospital, I mean."

His father moved across and leaned against the car. He didn't say anything.

Adam looked back into the black black sky. "I wanted ... I wanted to set her free."

"Set her free?"

Adam gulped and stood as straight as he could. But before he could say anything else, his dad spoke again.

"I think I know what you mean," he said. "You wanted to tell her that it was OK for her not to hang on. You wanted to tell her ... you wanted to tell her ..." He seemed unable to think of the words.

Adam watched him. His dad's head seemed to droop further and further forward.

"You wanted to ... tell her that you loved ..."

Adam's dad bent over and a sound came from him that Adam had never heard before. He had heard people talk about 'wailing' but he had never quite understood what that would sound like. But now he knew. It wasn't crying and it wasn't sobbing. It was something else. It was a sound of such sadness, a sound without hope and it cut through his own heart like a butcher's knife.

"Oh, Dad ... please don't cry," he said, and he ran over and hugged him. "It'll be OK, really it will."

"Oh, God, lovey ... I miss her so very, *very* much."

"I know, Dad. I know."

With his arms wrapped tightly around Adam's shoulders and his face in Adam's neck, his dad sobbed. It was as though a huge dam had been broken. He felt his dad's tears wet on his own skin.

"There," Adam said, "there there, it'll be OK." He held his dad as tightly as he could and breathed in the smoky smell in his hair.

"I just didn't think I had the strength," Adam's dad said, his voice muffled. And then he said, "Until tonight." He pulled himself up again and wiped his eyes with a crumpled hanky.

Adam stepped back and patted his dad's knee. It felt strange to be doing that, strange and awkward. But it also felt good somehow. He felt as though he was needed more than ever before. Maybe that was what being a knight was all about.

"Anyway, let's get you to bed." He reached over and ruffled Adam's hair and Adam felt like a child again. That, too, was a good feeling. It was, he knew, the way things should be ... the way they had to be. But he knew he would never forget, in all the years that lay ahead of him – even if he lived to be

45, those strange and sad few minutes when he had been in charge – in control.

"We've got a big day tomorrow," Adam's dad said as he walked with Adam to the house. The lights were on in the windows and the Christmas tree lights twinkled like little coloured stars. It looked welcoming. It looked more like home than Adam thought it had ever done. "We're going to need our rest."

When they went to bed, Adam stayed awake for a while to see if he would hear his dad crying. But the house was silent and more calm than it had felt in a very long time. Before he knew it, he was fast asleep.

****

"Rise and shine, lazybones!"

Adam turned over and screwed up his eyes at the sudden brightness.

His dad was pulling back the curtains.

He shuffled up in his bed and felt a lump under his bottom. He reached beneath the sheets and pulled out Buzz Lightyear, the spaceman's head twisted right around and one leg straight up against his arm. Adam moved the leg and head into their correct positions and sat Buzz next to him, wrapping the sheets around the two of them. "Brrr, it's cold!"

His dad came and sat on the bed and gave Adam a big smile. "Did you sleep OK?"

Adam nodded and then remembered what day it was. He looked around the room. In the corner, over by the door, was a big sack with the word 'Adam' stitched onto its side in red letters. Adam's mum had made that sack for him years ago and every Christmas he left it out for Father Christmas. "He's been!" Adam shouted.

His dad nodded. "Good job I remembered to put your sack out." He jabbed Adam in the tummy. "*You* forgot!"

Adam started to throw the sheets back, but his dad grabbed his arm and shook his head. "There's something I think we have to do before we can think of opening presents," he said.

Dad's face looks different this morning, Adam thought. My dad, James Best. Not just his dad but a man who existed in his own right. He looked stronger, in some way, sitting there on the edge of Adam's bed with the light from the window washing over him. His skin was puffy underneath his eyes but the greyness that had coloured his face these past months had vanished. Now he just looked tired. Tired but strong.

"What's that?" Adam said with a frown. He glanced across at the bulging sack, saw all the edges of the things it contained pushing

at the material. It was hard to think of
something that could be more important than
opening his presents.

"Well," Adam's dad said, relaxing his grip
on Adam's arm and running his hand through
Adam's hair. "Christmas is about giving as
well as receiving, yes?"

Adam nodded.

"So, I think we need to give a present to
Mum."

Adam made a face. He hadn't bought his
mother *anything* for Christmas. He had
saved up some of his weekly pocket money
and bought his dad a pair of socks from Next
but he had forgotten all about his mum. He
was about to tell his dad but his dad started
speaking again.

"We're going to set her free, just like you
said."

Adam gulped. "Can we do that?" In his mind, Adam saw him and his dad sneak into the hospital and up to his mum's room ... to pull the tube out from her throat. He didn't think they would be able to do it, not without being seen ... and then there was the problem of the beeping thing outside his mum's door. Maybe his dad didn't know about that. But his dad was nodding.

"I talked with the nurse last night," he said. "She was going to ask the special doctors to come in and do some tests on Mum, and ..."

"Tests?" Mum couldn't even speak, so how was she going to be able to do tests?

"The special doctors are going to see if ... they're going to see if your mum is able to breathe by herself. And if she isn't ..." Just for a second or two, Adam's dad's face seemed to cloud over. But it was only for a couple of seconds. "And if she isn't," he went on, "we're

going to let her go. We're going to set her
free."

"Is that her present?"

Adam's dad nodded. "That's her present."
He watched Adam and Adam watched him.
Adam felt he was expected to say something
but he didn't know what it was that he should
say.

"Are you OK with that?"

"Are you?" Adam said.

His dad seemed to think that over. Then
he said, "Yes, I am. I think it's the right
thing."

A single tear brimmed in Dad's eye. Adam
watched it form and watched it slide out and
roll down his dad's cheek. "It'll be OK," he
said. And he crept across to his dad.
Throwing his arms around his dad's neck,
Adam said, "We'll be OK."

Chapter 11
Letting Go

Adam's mum's room looked less scary in the daylight.

His dad had talked with two important-looking men for a good few minutes. One of the men, a tall, stern-looking man wearing a waistcoat, had asked his dad if his dad wanted to talk outside the room. And the two of them had turned to look at Adam. His dad had shaken his head. "No," he had told the man, "Adam is as much a part of this as I am."

The other man had nodded at that, and he had smiled. And then he had looked down at Adam and winked. Adam had tried to return the wink but he had never been very good at it. The result was that he closed both eyes and then opened them again a second later. That made the man smile.

What Adam's dad had said made Adam feel very important. So he listened very carefully to everything that was said. But not much of it made any sense to him, and, time after time, Adam felt his eyes glancing across at his mum's figure, her chest rising and falling,

Creak

Sigh

with the machine.

But the machine's voice said instead,

Gab

Gab

and Adam could hear his mum's voice saying it, the way she always used to do when Dad was on the phone talking with one of his friends from work. He could hear it so clearly that he looked around at the others to see if they had heard it too, but they just carried on talking. Mum had always said people were gabbing on when they were talking too much. It made Adam smile but he covered his mouth with his hand.

"Adam," Adam's dad said at last, "Doctor Brown says that Mum isn't going to be able to breathe without the machines. He says she'll never be able to come home again. She can go on like this," he waved an arm around the room, "perhaps for years, never able to speak to us, never able to see us and never able to ..."

"She's dead, isn't she?"

The nurse standing by the door gave Adam one of those looks, a mother's look, and a sad smile played across her lips. She started to nod her head.

"Yes," his dad said. "Mum's dead. But the machines are keeping her body breathing."

"But it's not Mum who's breathing, is it? The machines are breathing for her."

The tall doctor sighed, half smiled, and seemed to be about to say something. Then the other one, the one who had winked at Adam, sat on the chair and drew Adam towards him.

"Your mum was very badly hurt in the car crash, Adam," he said. "We were able to fix up the cuts and bruises on her body but there were cuts and bruises to your mum's brain as well. Bad ones ... cuts and bruises which have stopped your mum's brain from working. And those are the ones we haven't been able to fix.

96

"And when the brain isn't working," the doctor went on, "it can't send out any messages. It can't tell your mum when to breathe, it can't tell her when to eat ..."

"What the doctor is saying, lovey," Adam's dad said, "is they're never going to be able to get Mum well again."

Adam looked down at his feet and mumbled.

His dad leaned forward close to Adam's head. "What's that?" he whispered in Adam's ear.

Adam looked up. "Then we have to set her free," he said. "We have to let her go."

Adam's dad smiled and Adam could see he was holding back tears.

His dad stood up again and turned to the two doctors. "We want you to let her go." He put his hand on Adam's shoulder.

The tall doctor nodded and walked across to the chair behind the door. He lifted a brown folder, opened it and handed the folder to Adam's dad. Adam looked around at the faces in the room and then looked at his dad, who was reading the sheet of paper in the folder. "I'm sorry," Adam's dad said at last, looking around at the doctor, "but do you have a pen?"

"Of course." The tall doctor held out a shiny pen and Adam's dad took it and wrote something on the form. Then he closed the folder and handed it back to the doctor.

"Is it a long job?" he asked.

The doctor shook his head. "We just switch everything off," he said.

Adam and his dad looked across at the hi-fi set-up, which creaked and sighed,

Yes

Please

It seemed to say ...

Yes

Please

"Show me what to do," Adam's dad said.

The doctor started to say something, and the purple nurse stepped away from the wall behind the door.

But the shorter doctor, the one who had winked at Adam, raised a hand which stopped the purple nurse in her tracks. "Are you sure, Mr Best?" he asked. "Are you really sure you want to do this?"

Adam's dad said, "Is there any hope at all that she might get better?"

Both doctors shook their heads.

"Then, yes," Adam's dad said. "I'm sure."

Adam looked up at his father and saw someone else standing there. It was still his dad but yet it was someone else as well ... someone he didn't know. He saw a special side of his dad, a side that maybe didn't have to show itself much but which was always there just the same.

"Here," the doctor said, pointing to a single switch covered with a metal bar. He flipped the bar down. "That's all there is."

Adam's dad breathed in deeply and stepped across to the machine.

He reached out and placed his finger on the switch.

Then he looked across at the figure on the bed.

"Merry Christmas, sweetie," he said.

And he flicked the switch.

In that instant, Adam didn't see a man flicking a switch ...

He saw a man

But not all strength is physical strength

pulling a sword

If your cause is good, then you will prevail

out of a stone ...

Love

You

the machine said, its voice sounding faraway and dreamy.

And then it was silent.

Adam's mum's chest was no longer moving. Now she was truly still.

Adam's dad moved across and sat on the edge of the bed. He took hold of Mum's hand and rubbed his own hand along the back of it very gently. Then he placed her hand back by her side.

As he looked at his mum's face, Adam thought he saw the faintest movement ... a shadow, passing across her features and drifting away.

Although she did not look any different to the way she had looked only minutes earlier, there was now a peace about the figure in the bed. And as he was leaving the room with his dad, Adam saw that what he was looking at on the narrow hospital bed was little more than a photo. An image of something that had once been but was no more. The record of a time that had gone.

But memories – *real* memories – don't fade like old photos. You carry them in your head for always.

The machine would breathe again some day,

Creak

Sigh

for someone else, but Adam knew it wouldn't sound the same as it had done with his mum.

They went back through the hospital, the way they had come and, even though there were lots of people coming and going, everywhere seemed to be quiet ... silent ... as though the world was showing respect. Adam walked as straight and tall as his dad did. He felt that everyone knew what they had done ... and that everyone was very proud of them both.

Minutes later, they were outside in the mid-day watery sunshine.

Perhaps, Adam thought, he *was* the bravest of all the knights of old, strong of will and truth, and firm of purpose. But the man who walked beside him – the man who, even now, was hugging Adam close to his side ... that man was truly a *king*.

It started to snow.

Christmas Day was now really here.

Heading for home, Adam breathed in the cold and the promise of the future, and all the wonder and mystery it contained.

Parting is all we know of heaven,
And all we need of hell

Emily Dickinson (1830-1886)

Barrington Stoke would like to thank all its readers for commenting on the manuscript before publication and in particular:

Isabel Agnew
Anthony Bantolo
Anthea Beale
Robert Beck
Martin Carter
Michelle Cleghorn
Nick Coombe
Jamie Crook
Daniel Crossan
Reece Davidson
Kirsty Ellaway
Kirsteen Fraser
Sasha Gardner
Tom Hardiman
Paul Holden

Adam Hurd
Abby Inman
Gavin Johnson
Paul Johnson
Danny Jones
William Leigh-Firbank
Elaine McCall
Stephanie Pears
Emlyn Richards
Helen Taylor
Mrs Sangster
Eleanor Shakespeare
Jacqueline Wallington
Joyce Wilford
Ig Wilkinson

Become a Consultant!

Would you like to give us feedback on our titles before they are published? Contact us at the e-mail address below – we'd love to hear from you!

E-mail: info@barringtonstoke.co.uk
Website: www.barringtonstoke.co.uk

More Teen Titles!

Joe's Story by Rachel Anderson 1-902260-70-8
Playing Against the Odds by Bernard Ashley 1-902260-69-4
Harpies by David Belbin 1-84299-031-4
To Be A Millionaire by Yvonne Coppard 1-902260-58-9
Ring of Truth by Alan Durant 1-84299-033-0
Falling Awake by Viv French 1-902260-54-6
The Wedding Present by Adèle Geras 1-902260-77-5
Shadow on the Stairs by Ann Halam 1-902260-57-0
Alien Deeps by Douglas Hill 1-902260-55-4
Runaway Teacher by Pete Johnson 1-902260-59-7
No Stone Unturned by Brian Keaney 1-84299-034-9
Wings by James Lovegrove 1-84299-011-X
Clone Zone by Jonathan Meres 1-84299-009-8
The Dogs by Mark Morris 1-902260-76-7
A Kind of Magic by Catherine MacPhail 1-84299-010-1
All Change by Rosie Rushton 1-902260-75-9
The Blessed and The Damned by Sara Sheridan 1-84299-008-X

Barrington Stoke, 10 Belford Terrace, Edinburgh EH4 3DQ
Tel: 0131 315 4933 Fax: 0131 315 4934
E-mail: info@barringtonstoke.co.uk
Website: www.barringtonstoke.co.uk